CW01512709

When
the
War
Comes
In

When the War Comes In

Chris Callaghan

Illustrated by
Isabella Grott

Collins

Chapter 1
Friday
A visitor from the war

The battleship at the end of Jack's cobbled street sounded different to what he'd been expecting. Its engines rumbled with a low, broken growl, instead of the fierce, sharp roar he was used to. Everyone at Jack's school had been buzzing all day with rumours of a new visitor to the shipyard. Some had said that it was a German warship, and that the spring of 1944 was a perfect time for the start of an enemy invasion. He'd not believed them, but it was still a relief to see that the ship was British. He was more familiar with the sight and sounds of brand-new ships, growing up just a stone's throw away from the shipyard. Literally, a stone's throw away.

Jack and his friends would often chuck small rocks from the wall at the end of the street to hear them clang against steel hull panels, until angry shouts from the shipyard workers told them to stop. Then he would watch those ships sail off, ready for the fight that awaited them.

This was something different. The ship looked old but mighty. There were scorch marks around its impressive guns, and blackened dents along its grey steelwork. This ship had stories to tell. This was a real war veteran.

"She's a beauty, all right," said Mr Osbourne from number 12, limping towards him. "Just look at those lines of rivets. They did a fine job, whoever built her."

Jack nodded and asked, "What's she doing here? Another refit?"

He knew Mr Osbourne would know. "The Boss" always did. He'd been a crane operator at the yards for decades until a fall from the driver's cabin had damaged his legs. They made him General Manager after that, not wanting to lose him. "Best fall I've ever had," he always joked. Mr Osbourne retired just before the war started, and he was now the local air-raid warden, which gave him the perfect excuse to stick his nose in everyone's business.

"Quick repair work," he said. "One of the

artillery guns is getting replaced, there's scuffs to some of the externals, and a few bulkheads need welding. She was hit by the Luftwaffe not far from Malta."

Jack gasped. The Luftwaffe! He'd seen the newsreels at the Apollo cinema in Byker – before it was hit by a bomb and had to close – about the German air force attacking British ships.

"Tight deadline too, I hear," Mr Osbourne continued. "She must be needed somewhere sharpish. Your dad and his welding team will be doing plenty of extra hours. No Sunday off for him this week. Well – " He saluted the ship. "Welcome to Wallsend, HMS *Warspite*. We'll make you better than you ever were."

Hobbling off down the road, he added, "Say 'hello' to your mam from me, bonny lad."

"Aye, I will, Mr Osbourne," said Jack, pushing open his front door. He was hoping there was something to eat.

"This is Frank," said Dad, when he returned from the shipyard that night. He threw his haversack on a chair and headed to the kitchen. A young lad in a naval uniform, carrying a kit bag, peered in through the doorway and smiled.

"Oh!" said Mam, wiping her oil-stained hands on her apron, before offering one to the newcomer. "Pleased to meet you, Frank. I'm Mary and this is our Jack."

They all shook hands and Dad returned with two cups of water.

"Get that down you, lad," he said, offering one to Frank. "Parched, I am." After some hefty gulps, Dad continued, "Frank's going to be staying with us while we mend his rowing boat – you might've noticed it parked out there." Dad winked at Jack. "We normally deal with the bigger boats here, but I'm sure we can find some toy tools for your little plaything."

"Sit down here, Frank," said Mam, moving Dad's haversack and placing it on the floor, "and just ignore Norman. It's a fine ship you've got there. What is it you do onboard?"

"I'm an anti-aircraft gun operator," said Frank, easing into the big, worn armchair, clearly enjoying its softness. "And that *rowing boat* took part in the Battle of Jutland in the last war," Frank continued. "We call her the *Grand Old Lady*."

"Well," grinned Dad, pointing at Mam, "this grand old lady makes anti-aircraft guns in a factory just up the road. The mobile ones, not ones like yours."

"Gun operator?" Jack gasped. He perched on the arm of the chair. "Mr Osbourne said you've been in a battle with the Luftwaffe. Was it a Junkers or a

Messerschmitt?" Jack was interested in military aircraft as well as ships; he knew all the makes and models.

"A squadron of Focke-Wulfs," replied Frank.

"Did you shoot any down?" asked Jack, wide-eyed. "Did anyone get killed?"

"No, no," said Mam, waving her hands about. "We don't have those conversations here. Leave the lad alone; he must be exhausted."

Dad loudly finished another cup of water, and added, "The navy are giving some of their boys a bit of shore leave, and Frank's one of the lucky few. The rest are still onboard doing whatever it is that they do. So, I mentioned that we had a spare bed in the old Collier household."

Dad turned to a framed photo on the mantlepiece of a young man in uniform. Everyone followed his gaze. "I hope that was all right?" he added, in a more sombre tone.

"Of course it is," Mam said, turning her gaze from the photograph. "You can have our Gordon's bed. It's all ready. It's always ready for whenever he comes home. But you'll be very welcome to it for – " She looked at Dad.

"Just a few days," he reassured her. "The little rowing boat out there has to leave the dock no later than midnight on Sunday with the *utmost urgency*, so we're told."

"Are you going straight back to Malta to get them Focke-Wulfs?" asked Jack.

"We don't need to know any details, young man," said Mam, in her telling-off voice.

Dad tapped the side of his nose. "Loose lips, sink ships, and all that."

He gestured for Frank to get up. "Haway then. I'll show you the lie of the land."

It was a squeeze for all four of them in the kitchen. Dad showed Frank how to turn the tap on and off as if he'd never operated one before. Pots and pans were handed back and forth for Dad to show off the welding he'd done to repair them, making them unwieldy and heavy. Banging one off a wall, he said, "They might not be pretty, but they're the strongest pots you'll find anywhere."

Black dust jumped about the kitchen with each thud and the deafening clashes made everyone wince.

"Do you really have to?" said Mam, rolling her eyes and ushering them out into the back.

The yard was littered with stacked wooden crates filled with all kinds of rusting metal parts and tools, all kept cool by the shadow of the looming battleship.

"This is our shelter," said Mam, pointing to the brick structure taking up most of the yard. "Just in case we need it."

"I built it myself," said Dad. He banged its roof with the pan he was still holding. It clanged as if he'd just bashed a battleship. "That's three inches of steel armour plating. I bet it'll withstand a direct hit."

"Well, let's hope we never have to find out," tutted Mam.

"Now the most important room in the house – "

Dad announced grandly. "The netty."

They smiled at Frank's confused face, until Dad opened a door revealing the outside toilet.

"Made with pipework from the great *Mauretania* herself," Dad said. "The biggest and fastest ship there ever was … once upon a time. And built right here on Tyneside." Dad puffed out his chest and admired the bulky tangle of metal plumbing that'd been welded and riveted together. In a further demonstration of how a toilet worked, Dad pulled a chain thick enough to carry a ship's anchor. There was a moment's pause … then a gurgle … then a clank and a twang … then a crashing of water that sounded like you were at the end of Tynemouth pier on a stormy day. Frank stepped back as the place shook and water furiously cascaded into the toilet bowl.

"Never pull the chain while you're still sitting on it," instructed Dad, with a wink, "or you'll get sucked out into the river."

Frank's face showed he wasn't sure whether to believe Dad or not, but he'd be a fool to take that chance.

Jack opened another door next to the toilet. "This is the coal shed," he explained. "Don't get these two doors mixed up!"

"I'll try my best to remember that!" laughed Frank.

Chapter 2
War stories

Supper was potatoes, leeks and carrots. Everyone helped with the peeling and chopping, and while the vegetables boiled, the household duties were shared out, even to Frank. Being so close to the shipyard meant a constant battle with an industrial level of dust and grime. All the surfaces had a dark, gritty coating. Wiping an area wouldn't make it clean, but the coating would be less thick than areas not wiped. Plates, cups and cutlery were washed after they were used and given another wipe just before they were needed again. Windows were only cleaned when sunlight shone through them, highlighting how dirty they were. That didn't happen much as there was usually a huge ship blocking the sun.

Huddled around the small kitchen table,

they tucked into their vegetables with ravenous excitement. Dad always slurped because he'd lost most of his front teeth after an accident at work. He was happy to point out his broken nose and scar running down a cheek from the same incident.

Even though everyone was exhausted, Mam kept the polite conversation going by asking Frank about his home. Tales of a little village in Essex, surrounded by beautiful countryside, seemed

a long, long way from the grey streets of Tyneside. Jack and his parents were particularly interested in Frank's Anderson shelter, which had been dug into the family's flowerbed, mainly because they all dreamt of living in a house with a garden.

"The *Anson* was built here," said Dad, proudly.

"HMS *Anson*?" gasped Frank, with clear amazement. "You built her here?"

Dad held up his heavily callused hands, ingrained with dirt, to show Frank he had two missing fingers.

"With my own fair hands."

Mam groaned. "I'm sure a few others helped you too. Frank doesn't want to hear any more battleship stories after being cooped up on one for months. Let's get all this washed up then Jack can show him his room."

"I'll tell you all about it another time," Dad promised Frank.

"This one's mine and that's yours," said Jack, showing Frank the beds. "It's got clean sheets ready for Gordon whenever he comes back."

"Gordon's your brother?" Frank asked. "That's a photograph of him on your mantlepiece?"

Jack nodded. "He joined the army last year. He's in the 3rd Infantry Division, not long out of training. We haven't seen him in ages, but we think he's still in the country. He didn't say much in his last letter."

"I'm not too good at writing letters either," Frank admitted. "I never know what to say. I'm sure that's the same for your brother."

Outside, the clanking and groaning of metal upon metal, with short bursts of hammering and riveting, caught Frank's attention. The *Warspite* was dotted with sparks of fiery light.

"Are there people still working this late?" Frank asked.

"Aye, they'll be there all night, probably," said Jack, turning to perch on the windowsill. "They've

started the welding already. That one's the Titan with the jib moving," he continued, pointing to the huge crane swivelling with a mighty, gradual grace towards the warship. "They'll use that to refit the guns. It's a beast; it can lift anything. And the skinny crane's called Hector. It's quicker and handles the lighter stuff."

But Jack wanted to talk about something else. "So where have you been? I mean, if you're allowed to tell me."

"Just the Mediterranean lately, helping out with the Allied landings in Italy," Frank replied.

Jack had seen that on recent newsreels, too, which they'd started showing at the Memorial Hall up the road. He couldn't believe he was sharing a room with someone who'd been there. "That squadron of Focke-Wulfs must have been an impressive sight."

Jack also hid news articles and torn out pages from magazines on military vehicles in his desk at school and read them when he should have been doing equations.

"*Did* you shoot any?" asked Jack. Mam wasn't there to stop him asking this time.

"We clipped a few," Frank told him. "But they're so fast. The ship got badly shot up and we were supposed to be heading to Rosyth in Scotland for major repairs, but we got new orders, and here we are."

"I want to join the infantry like Gordon and fight next to him," Jack said. "I'm 14 next year and I've heard some 15-year-olds have sneaked in. So maybe it won't be long before I can be a part of it and do my bit."

"Don't you worry about that until you're older." Frank yawned deeply. "This war's not going anywhere." He lay back on the bed and a few moments later he was snoring loudly. Jack smiled. Frank snored just like Gordon. It used to be something that drove Jack up the wall, and he'd spend most of the night with his head under a pillow. Now he realised how much he missed it.

Jack crept downstairs for some water, knowing there was a good chance Mam and Dad would be asleep as usual in the big chair. Indeed, they were! He turned off the radio and pulled a blanket over them. They stirred slightly but didn't wake up. Instead, they huddled closer, holding each other's hands. Their fingers had cuts and scratches from work, and their fingernails were broken and bruised. It was hard to tell whose fingers were whose.

Chapter 3
Saturday
Toon Army

Jack woke earlier than normal for a Saturday. He was used to the general banging and clattering going on in the yards, but it seemed even more frantic than normal. The foghorns blaring away didn't help either. Mam and Dad had gone to work, and Frank's bed was empty. There were a lot of people milling about on the street, so Jack pulled on his clothes and joined them.

Warspite's great guns poked through the murky grey fog that often rolled in off the Tyne on a crisp morning. One of the guns was now dangling from the Titan crane. The outline of the warship blurred in the mist, making her look as if she was creeping out from a dream or, more likely, a nightmare. The low, booming foghorn seemed to come from the heart of the battleship itself, as a forewarning of impending doom. Jack shuddered.

News of the arrival had clearly spread around town and a sizeable crowd had gathered to look at the battleship. There was always interest in what was going on in the yards. On launch days, the surrounding streets were packed out. Jack had to push and shove through the masses just to get in and out of his front door.

Among the locals there were new faces in navy uniforms, leaning along the long wall at the

end of the street, on the bank or in groups, happily loitering. They were all reading newspapers and were full of chatter and laughs. One of them gave Jack a wave and came running towards him. It was Frank and he had a huge grin on his face.

"This is the life," he said, with a mouthful of something. "New newspapers. Not old newspapers, but new ones. And pies!" He laughed and waved the remains of some mangled pastry. "They're giving them away on the High Street. Pies for breakfast … that's my new favourite thing."

Jack knew that the High Street shopkeepers did fundraising for visitors from the yards, and pies were always popular. He wasn't likely to get a free one as he wasn't in uniform, which was a shame because pies for breakfast sounded great.

A football bounced next to them. Frank spun on his heels and caught it under his foot with impressive skill.

"It's been ages since I've played some footy," he said, flicking the ball from foot to foot.

Jack felt the same. He hadn't had a game since his brother left. They'd always kicked a ball around the street together or did keepy-uppies in the backyard. It wasn't the same without him.

Terry, Cliff and Ann, the kids from number 21, gestured for their ball to be booted back, but Frank was enjoying himself too much. The kids came over. "Us against you two?" Ann grinned.

"I've heard you Geordies like your football," said Frank. "Let's see if you're any good at it."

Dribbling the ball between the three kids, Frank sped off along the road. Terry, Cliff and Ann immediately chased him. Jack sighed, not wanting to join in, but Mam had told him to show their guest a good time. So, reluctantly, he followed.

Terry, Cliff and Ann were small but speedy, and easily intercepted Frank's passes to Jack. Jack knew he had to up his game if he didn't want to be embarrassed – he'd never live it down if the young kids won. It didn't take long for his competitive spirit to bring some effort and, eventually, fun to his playing. Even though the kids were outclassed by Frank and Jack, their smiles and giggles never stopped.

It wasn't long before the general pass-about was noticed by others, and goalposts made of bricks and stones from the crumbling wall at the end of the street were soon in position. The fog was returning to the Tyne, but even the sun made an appearance to shimmer on the cobbles. The crowd had thinned out, but they turned their attention from the battleship to the football. Uniformed sailors, who'd finished their pies and newspapers, joined in the game, to the cheers of the watching throng.

More local kids and some grown-ups joined in too, until there was a natural split of teams – navy boys versus local lads and lasses. Jack was now on the opposite team to Frank. They exchanged steely grins. Frank had the ball and Jack tackled him hard to get it back. Too hard. They clattered together and Frank tumbled onto the cobbles.

A sharp ear-piercing whistle blew, making everyone freeze.

"Foul!" came a shout from the sidelines. It was Mr Osbourne with his air-raid warden gear.

He limped with determination onto the makeshift pitch. "You all right, lad?" he asked. Frank laughed and Jack pulled him up with a sheepish look.

"I'm fine," he smiled, ruffling Jack's hair. "Blimey, you take no prisoners!"

24

Mr Osbourne nodded and shouted, "Free kick. Get ten yards back, young Master Collier."

The game continued under the watchful eye of the Boss. Bedroom windows along the street opened, from which black and white scarves for the local team, known as "the Toon" were enthusiastically waved.

This feels like a proper match, Jack thought.

The thud of every kick and every bounce of the ball echoed off the *Warspite*'s huge metallic hull, making the street sound like the Toon's home ground of St James' Park itself. There were "Ooos" and "Ahhs" from the crowd, especially when the ball battered off the wall close to a window. Mr Lachut from number 34 opened his front door after a ball bounced off it, thinking someone had knocked. His initial concern over such a heavy clatter at the door quickly turned into keen shouts of "Boot it, man, boot it!".

The game was played at a furious pace. Jack was enjoying himself, but he was frustrated that he'd not yet scored. His heart pounded as the ball landed at his feet. A line of navy lads formed in front of him, making a straight dash for the goal impossible. A long run around them was an option, but Jack knew that dribbling wasn't his strength. The men ran towards him, and he was annoyed with himself for hesitating too long. Then an idea struck him.

Jack was in front of his own front door, and he pushed it open. With a flick of his foot, the ball bounced into his hallway and down towards the kitchen. Following the ball in, he tried to close the door quickly behind him, but a sailor's boot stopped it shutting completely. Hearing the door crash open, he raced through the kitchen, nudging the ball along the wooden floor, and out into the back yard. He couldn't stop giggling, and he could hear the panting, laughing and thunder of feet following him through his house.

He flicked open the gate from the yard into the back lane, where he had more space to kick the ball a little further each time, and he soon made it to the end house and around the corner. The pack of excited footballers weren't far behind him.

Jack dribbled the ball round the corner, and

returned to the street, which was now almost empty of players. The crowd cheered and clapped.

The opposition goalkeeper couldn't see Jack approaching from behind. Just as the mass of players re-entered the street, Jack got in front of the goal. He turned, and booted the ball between the brick goalposts, much to the surprise of the goalkeeper. The crowd erupted in delight until another sharp ear-piercing whistle brought silence.

Jack's shoulders slumped; he was expecting a shout of "Foul". Instead, Mr Osbourne hollered, "GOOOOAL!"

Everyone cheered and clapped. Even those in uniform. Jack felt like he'd scored the winner in the FA Cup Final.

"I've never seen that tactic before," Frank panted, shaking Jack's hand. "You Geordies definitely know how to play."

That seemed like a good point to end the match. No one knew exactly what the score was, but it really didn't matter. Jack gave the ball back to Terry, Cliff and Ann who held it like it was the actual World Cup trophy.

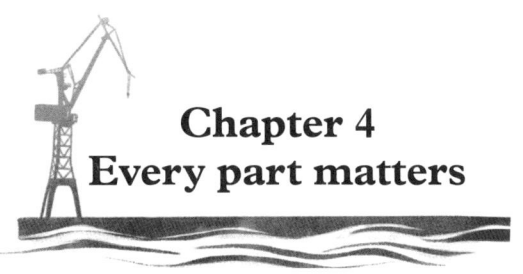

Chapter 4
Every part matters

"What's happened to the door?" shouted Dad, when he got home from work later that day. Jack and Frank came downstairs while Mam appeared from the kitchen. Dad opened and closed the front door, showing it had come off its bottom hinges and was only hanging on from the top.

"I came in through the back, so I never noticed," said Mam.

"Ah, yeah," said Jack, realising what must have happened. "It's a football related accident."

"It's my fault; I started it all," Frank said.

Jack added, "No, it was me who – "

Dad interrupted them both. "Football related?

You've been playing football in the house?"

"Not completely," Jack said.

"Mostly outside," confirmed Frank.

"And did you both score?" asked Dad.

"Frank scored a few. He's a canny player."

"Thanks, mate," said Frank, "but Jack here scored the best one. The crowd went wild!"

"The crowd?" laughed Dad. "Well, I suppose that's something." He crouched down to look at the damage. "Right, I'll get this fixed before I sit down. 'Cos if I sit down, I'll not get back up."

Jack and Frank were keen to help, as it was their fault the door was broken. The bottom hinge had snapped, so they rummaged around in the backyard for the wooden crate full of screws, bolts, washers and general bits and bobs. Dad got his tools and some bits of wood to shove under the door.

Jack and Frank weren't sure which screws they needed, so they brought the whole crate through and sat it in the hallway. Each screw they pulled

out to offer Dad was either too long, too short or too narrow. Dad wanted the precise fit for every hole and replaced some of the older screws whether they were broken or not. This went on for ages and Jack became bored. With only one final screw needed, which they were struggling to find, Jack said, "It's only one screw. There are already loads of others. One missing screw won't make any difference."

Dad stopped what he was doing and looked at Jack. Mam peered out from the kitchen and grimaced.

"Everything," said Dad, calmly and carefully, "and I mean *everything*, is only as strong as its weakest part. No matter how small, or how big, or how important or unimportant any single part might seem ... every part matters."

Mam joined in with the search, but no one could find the right one. Another crate was brought in and tipped out onto the floor. All kinds of metal widgets, doodahs and whatnots spilt out.

"What about this?" said Jack, holding up a shiny screw and really, really hoping it was suitable.

"Perfect," said Dad. He held the screw for a moment so they could all see it. "Every ... part ... matters."

The hinge was carefully screwed into place and Dad opened and closed the door a few times, while everyone else scraped everything back into the crates.

"Better than it ever was," smiled Dad.

"I'll dish up," said Mam.

"I'm starving!" Jack and Frank said together.

Dad arched his back. "I definitely need a sit down. It's been a long old day."

Just then, the air-raid siren whined.

"Fill the bottles, someone," groaned Dad. He picked up a couple of cushions and a newspaper from an armchair and switched off the lights.

Jack was already at the kitchen sink filling milk bottles from the tap. He then grabbed a grey canvas bag and the remains of a candle. "Will this be enough?" he asked, showing Dad the waxy blob in his hand.

Dad shrugged. "It'll have to be."

Mam handed Jack a lump of cheese which he placed in the bag. "Where's Frank?"

"Is he in the shelter already?" Dad went to check but came back shaking his head. They called out Frank's name and peered into the gloomy darkness. Jack was about to look upstairs but noticed something under the kitchen table. It was Frank.

"Haway," laughed Jack, crouching down. "The shelter's in the backyard, remember?" But Frank didn't move.

Dad bent down. "Hey, bonny lad. If it was up to me, I'd stay in the house as well. It'll be just another false alarm."

But Mam wasn't messing about. She grabbed Frank, and heaved him out from under the table, before herding everyone into the yard. Everyone in town was familiar with Mam's strength. There were tales of her winning tug-of-war and arm-wrestling competitions against yard workers and miners during summer fairs before the war. This reputation had grown during her time at the armament factory, where she could load and stack more ammunition shells than anyone else. It was a strength that she rarely showed off, but everyone knew it was there.

The shipyard was in blackout due to the air raid, but the work carried on. Tight deadlines often meant that the workers couldn't have the safety of a shelter, and the darkness made everything more dangerous. Cranes moving huge steel plates would sometimes crash into buildings or scaffolding, or the vessel they were building, or the workers themselves.

Warspite's imposing silhouette loomed over their homemade shelter as the siren continued to drone and Mam hurried them inside.

Passing the cushions around, they slid into their bunks. Dad and Mam on the top ones, with Jack and Frank underneath. Dad lit the candle and opened the newspaper. Jack placed the bottles of water against the wall so they wouldn't get kicked over and rummaged in the bag for a packet of crackers, while Mam snapped off chunks of cheese for everyone. Dad refused the offered cheese with a grunt.

"I should've stayed at work," he grumbled. "I only came back for me tea."

When the shipyard had priority tasks to be completed, not only did the men and women continue to work during air raids, but the workers

were locked on site for days or weeks at a time. Only those who lived just outside the yards were allowed home during the day and night for brief periods.

"We promised Gordon we'd use the shelter, so we're using it," Mam sighed. "Do I really need to say that every time?"

Dad tightened his grip on the newspaper and muttered, "Waste of time."

Jack knew it was common for some people to stay in their homes and take the risk. At the start of the war there had been many more air raids with plenty of bombs dropping along the Tyne. The shipyards and factories were a prime target. In a town not far away, a single bomb had hit a shelter with 200 factory workers inside and more than 100 of them died. Faith that the shelters would save them lessened after that. Fewer air raids had occurred recently, but the threat never disappeared. When Gordon left home, Mam had made him promise he'd be careful, and in return he made them promise to use the shelter.

An awkward silence descended until after a while, Frank blurted out, "I don't want to go!" It was the first thing he'd said for ages.

"Don't want to go where, bonny lad?" asked Dad.

Frank sat up on his bunk, visibly shaking. "I don't want to go … back to the war."

Chapter 5
The war comes home

"**I** can't keep doing it," said Frank, as Jack handed him a bottle of water. Frank tried to take it, but his hands were shaking so much Jack took it back. "I can't keep doing it," said Frank, again. "When the alarms go off onboard," he continued, in almost a whisper, "all I want to do is hide. Hide from the aircraft or the U-boats. But I can't. I have to go up top."

The words flowed out of him, and no one tried to stop them. "I have to get to my post. It's what I have to do. It's what I'm trained to do. I have to look for the enemy. To turn towards the enemy. I've seen those fighters heading straight towards me. I've seen the flashes of gunfire coming at me." He sniffed hard. "I've felt the bullets whooshing past. Heard them smash into the ship. Smelt the burning metal. But it's all the wrong way around. We should be running away from danger, not going towards it."

Everyone was silent.

"My mate Billy got hit," he continued. "We'd gone through training together. His gun post was to the aft. I'd been with him in the galley just before the alarm went. He'd stuffed his face with so much food he couldn't chew it." Frank smiled. "He was a daft one, all right. But he made us laugh. And then he was gone."

Jack, Mam and Dad glanced at each other. No one knew what to say.

"We've been told to write a letter home," Frank continued, his voice becoming shakier, "before we depart from Tyneside. We were told to *resolve any family disputes*. I'm worried this will be the last letter I ever write. You see … I think something big is going to happen."

They sat for a while, motionless and silent, until Dad said, "I just can't imagine – " But his voice trailed off.

"We see the reports on the newsreels and in the papers," said Mam, "but it feels so distant, so separate from our lives."

"But you're right there," whispered Jack. "In the thick of it."

Dad jumped down from the bunk, took a blanket, and draped it around Frank, giving his shoulder a firm squeeze. Frank pulled it tightly around himself.

Dad frowned. "I'm sorry but I've really got to get back to work. I promised Sam and Kev I'd check one of their bulkhead refits. I've been longer than I should. Get your head down, lad. You'll be safe here."

Dad left, saying he'd see everyone in the morning. Mam followed him out, saying she'd only be a few minutes. Jack watched Frank curl back up on his bunk and heard Mam and Dad talking outside. He opened the door of the shelter just enough to hear.

"It must've been the air raid that set him off," whispered Mam. "There must be all sorts of alarms and sirens going off on a battleship. Especially with all he's been through."

"I don't know if I can do it again," muttered Dad, his voice soft and shaky. "I can't say goodbye to another young lad going off to war. It's not right. It's not fair. It should be me, not them."

"But what can we do?" asked Mam.

"We've got to do something," said Dad. "Imagine if this was our Gordon."

Mam clapped a hand over her mouth to stifle a cry.

"We'd hope that someone would look after him, wouldn't we?" Dad continued.

In the darkness, Jack could just make out the shape of his parents holding each other. Glancing back at Frank, he wondered if Gordon was somewhere … curled up … and afraid.

A couple of hours later, the "all clear" sounded. No bombs had been heard, and Mam, Frank and Jack shuffled out of the shelter, tired and fed up. The lights in the shipyard burst into life and the *Warspite* appeared like magic out of the darkness. Barrage balloons bobbed in the sky above. They'd been raised up as part of the air raid procedures. The nearest one to their house was fondly known as "Lucy" and Mam had always reassured Jack that Lucy was watching over them.

"Shall we wait for a bit and see?" asked Jack. "You know, like we used to do."

Mam smiled and nodded. "We can't wait too long, though. It's late." She flicked on the kitchen light, which lit up the backyard, while Jack climbed up onto the shelter roof.

Standing as if on a stage, and illuminated by the spotlight, Jack stared at the battleship as he moved his arms slowly up and down at his sides. The minutes ticked by, but he kept going until his arms began to ache. Just when he was about to stop, a figure on the deck of the warship moved their arms in the same way. Jack jumped up and down and excitedly waved back.

"Right!" sniffed Mam, with a quivery smile. "It's definitely bedtime now."

"Was that your dad you were waving to?" asked Frank later, as he pulled up the blankets.

Jack nodded. "Aye. It's just something we used to do when I was younger, after Dad had that accident. He got hit by a metal sheet hanging from a crane. It did that damage to his face, you know, his teeth and the scar." Frank nodded. "He lost a few fingers and broke some bones. He was unconscious for ages, and we weren't sure if he was going to die or not. But he didn't die, obviously, and even though he hadn't fully recovered, he had to go back to work because we needed the money. Me mam was worried about him, so she made him promise he'd wave at us whenever he got the chance. She used to sit by the wall at the top of the bank, or in the backyard if it was late, for hours. I'd be asleep on her lap, but she wouldn't go to bed until she'd seen him. It was just to make sure he was all right."

Jack's mind drifted back to his brother and he wondered if he was *all right*. When they'd taken Gordon to the train station the day he left for the army, Jack hadn't said anything to him. He'd stood on the platform staring at his shoes. Gordon had tried to speak to him and shake hands, but Jack had ignored him. He hadn't wanted him to go. It was only when the train started moving that Jack realised how selfish he was being. But it was too late. He chased the train as far as he could along the platform and watched until it disappeared down the tracks. Every day since he'd regretted it. Now there was someone else in Gordon's bed. "Are you all right?" he asked.

But Frank just said, "Night," quietly, and turned to face the wall.

Lying there, as the clank and whir of the shipyard and the low whistle of the wind blowing through the barrage balloon cables gently filled the room, Jack wondered what to say. He wanted to say something helpful. Instead, he waited, hoping to hear Frank snoring to know that he'd settled into a comfortable sleep.

But the snoring never came.

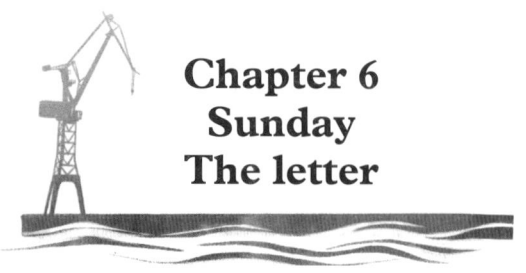

Chapter 6
Sunday
The letter

Jack heard Frank get up early. He followed him downstairs and found him standing at the front window gazing at the battleship. All its huge guns were in place and the Titan crane had backed away. A dawn chorus of hammering, but no riveting, suggested repairs were coming to an end. Jack offered Frank some breakfast, but it was refused with a slow shake of the head.

Suddenly, the front door burst open.

"Right," said Dad, rushing in with Mam, "we've been thinking."

"We've got family in Northumberland, up in the countryside," said Mam, looking at Jack. "You know, the Morelands in Bellingham. They're good people. We were going to send you off to them a few years back when the air raids got bad, remember?"

Dad put a hand on Frank's shoulder. "So … if you want … you can go there, and they'll look after you. You can wear some of Gordon's clothes and Mr Tomkins from the grocer's will take you."

Frank bowed his head and ran a hand through his hair.

Mam added, "Mr Tomkins is a kind man. He had a son in the army, until … well … he just understands."

"He goes up to the country to get stock for the shop," said Dad, "and he's going this morning."

Jack's head was spinning. "But what about the navy? They'll come and get him. He'll get into trouble."

Dad shrugged his shoulders. "We won't tell them where he's gone. I'll say there's been a mix up, or something. We'll deal with the consequences. And by then, the ship will have sailed."

"But Frank could go to prison," said Jack.

"Look," said Mam, wringing her hands, "we're not saying this is perfect. But if Frank doesn't want to get back on that ship, then we'll do all we can to make sure he doesn't."

Just then a few "hellos" sounded from the hallway.

"Sorry to barge in, Mrs Collier." It was Mrs Lachut from across the road. Her husband was with her, and they both grimaced at the solemn scene they'd interrupted. "We've just been to the Memorial Hall. We made some biscuits for the boys on the boat."

Mr Lachut nodded.

"They're collecting donations there. Anyway, Mrs Ferris from the other side of the High Street asked us to pass this on." Mrs Lachut held out a letter and offered it to Mam. "It got delivered there by mistake. They've got two lads overseas in the military and a lass down south working in operations or something, and this got mixed in with theirs. Lots of letters being delivered lately, so I heard. Something must be going on."

Mam took the letter. "It's from Gordon," she gasped.

"Hope everything's all right," said Mr Lachut, as they headed back out. "This war asks too much from our young, doesn't it."

"Very kind of you to bring it round," called out Dad.

"No bother, pet," said Mrs Lachut. "I wish there was more we could do to help." And they were gone.

Mam gripped the letter, staring at it intensely.

"Well, open it," Dad whispered. Mam shook her head and handed it to him. Then Dad stood motionless, staring at it until Jack took it from him. He tore impatiently at the envelope and slid out the paper.

"*Dear Mam, Dad and … Skinny Legs,*" Jack read. He rolled his eyes but smiled along with everyone else. "*I'm all right and still in England. Don't worry, I'm eating lots. Food's not as good as home but there's loads of it.*"

Mam sniffed and nodded.

"*I'm sorry that I haven't written more often. It's just been so busy. We've been given some time to write home and it's the quietest the tent has been since we got here. We haven't been told much but it feels like something's going on.*" Jack took a deep breath before continuing, "*Something big.*"

All eyes fell on Frank, and they remembered the same words he'd uttered the night before.

"*But,*" Jack swallowed hard and continued reading slowly, "*we're trained and we're ready. If I'm honest, I am nervous. We all are. But I'm with a bunch of canny lads. Our sergeant is from Sunderland, if you can believe that?*"

Dad raised his eyebrows making Jack smile. Sunderland was a few miles south of the river and their football teams were firm rivals.

Jack continued. *"In spite of that, he's a decent bloke and we'd follow him to the ends of the earth. I talk to him about football, but – "* Jack paused again, *"I'm missing my kickabouts with Jack. I'm missing you all. I even miss Dad's shipyard stories."*

Dad grinned and Mam let out a laugh, which turned into a sharp gasp as Jack read the next line. *"I especially miss the sound of Mam's laugh, and hope to hear that again one day. But there are things I need to do first. We're all ready for what happens next. Ready to fight for our homes and our families. I'm very proud to be a part of the 3rd Infantry Division, but I'm even more proud to be a Collier. Keep yourselves safe. Love, Gordon."*

Mam reached out for the letter. She ran her fingers over the words, and let out a little sob, which she tried to hide with a laugh. Everyone else stood in silence, lost in their own thoughts.

A sharp blast of a horn sounded from outside, shattering the calmness and making them all flinch.

"They're testing out the systems," Frank told them.

"All repairs will be finished this afternoon," said Dad. "The yard will meet its deadline with time to spare … like we always do. It'll be out of the Tyne before midnight." He turned to Frank. "But you've got another option, bonny lad. So, get yourself upstairs and changed, and we'll have you in Mr Tompkins' van and on your way to the countryside."

It was a momentous decision for Frank. His eyes were wide and red, and his face was pasty. He looked at each of them for an answer.

Jack nodded, "I think you should."

Mr Osbourne appeared in the hallway, and Mam whispered, "It's as busy as a train station in here!"

"Just in case you don't already know," Mr Osbourne said, "they're wanting spare hands in the yards to get everything cleared."

Dad nodded. "We're all heading there soon."

There were loud footsteps on the landing upstairs. Frank didn't know they had a visitor – if he came down and said something, their secret plan would be ruined. Dad tried to usher Mr Osbourne out. He was a decent man, but he lived by the rules and wouldn't tolerate something as extreme as desertion.

"I'm sure there are others that will help out as well, Mr Osbourne," said Mam, a lot louder than she needed to, in the hope Frank would hear. "Maybe the Morgans at number 28?"

But Mr Osbourne came further into the room and picked up the photo of Gordon from the mantlepiece. "They grow up so fast, don't they? It seems like only yesterday I was helping him mend a puncture on his little three-wheeler. Have you heard from him lately?"

Mam waved the letter. "Just got this. Still in England … for now."

The clatter of boots on the wooden hallway floor made everyone turn. Frank stood at the door in full uniform, holding his kit bag.

"But – " Jack said, before he stopped himself. Why was Frank in uniform?

"There's a grand sight," said Mr Osbourne, admiringly. "You ready for the off then, lad? Ready to serve your king and country?"

Frank looked at them. "If Gordon's ready … I'm ready."

Jack could see Mam and Dad trying not to look surprised.

"Good lad," Mr Osbourne said, and left to knock on more doors.

Once he'd left, they gasped out the air they hadn't realised they were holding in.

"Are you sure about this, pet?" asked Mam. "I mean, really, really sure?"

Frank nodded, but it was Jack who wasn't sure. He'd been looking forward to visiting him in the countryside. Maybe sharing a room with him again and playing football on the endless fields they had up there.

"I've got to report back onboard now," said Frank. Everyone froze open-mouthed, thinking this was "goodbye". "But I'll get some time before we set sail, and I was wondering if I could call in and say a proper goodbye … if that's all right?"

Jack nodded while Mam said, "Aye, aye, of course, pet. We'll do you some tea. We'll find something nice."

Dad had been standing silent, silhouetted in the window, and added quietly, "You're always welcome here, bonny lad."

Chapter 7
A surprise package

Once Frank had gone, Mam looked round the kitchen.

"We've got nothing in," she said. "I haven't been to the shops for days. I haven't had time. It's a Sunday; who knows where I'm going to get a plate full of decent food for the lad."

They readied themselves to get to the yards to help out. Even Jack was allowed in under Mam's close supervision. Mam called out to Dad from the front door to get him moving, but he was still in the front room. Going back in, she was ready to shout at him to hurry up, but the silence from the room made Jack also return and peep in at the door.

Dad was still standing by the window with his head bowed. Mam held one of Dad's hands then wiped something from his face.

"I know, I know," she said quietly. "But he's made his decision. There's nothing we can do for any of them while they're out there, but we can do something for them while they're here. We need to be strong for him. For them all."

Dad shook his head and Mam let out a little laugh. "You're the strongest man I know."

They put their arms around each other, and Jack joined them. For a while they hugged in silence.

That evening, Jack, Mam and Dad turned the corner back into their street, feeling utterly exhausted. It'd been hard work helping to move equipment, crane harnesses and tools off the ship, and clear the areas around it.

"What's that?" asked Jack, pointing at their front door. On the step was a small parcel and a couple of bottles. On closer inspection, they saw the package had "For Frank" written on it.

In the kitchen, they laid the package on the table. It was wrapped in pages of the latest edition of *Knitting for Victory* and when they unfolded it, some potatoes rolled out, a cabbage and a beautiful, thick steak. Jack had never seen a cut of meat like it.

"There's enough here for all of us," gasped Dad, but Mam pointed at the words written on the wrapper. Dad sighed, "So what are we going to have?"

"Bread, maybe? There are crackers. That'll have to do 'till the shops open tomorrow," Mam replied.

"Who's it from, do you think?" asked Jack.

Mam shook her head. "I mentioned to some

of the girls about Frank. Maybe Jackie? She's got an uncle who runs the butchers in Howdon."

"Two bottles of cherryade too," smiled Jack.

"One for Frank and one for you," Mam smiled back at him.

Jack had an idea and made them all one of his special suppers: a hot beefy drink made with stock cubes, each with broken crackers floating in it. They sat round the kitchen table spooning in mouthfuls of soggy, beefy lumps of cream crackers. After a busy day, it was glorious.

After their tea, they moved the kitchen table into the front room, as it was going to be Frank's last meal with them. This was something they only did on special occasions, such as Christmas, or when Auntie Delia from the posh end of town came for tea. The fancy plates had even been washed. There were only three plates now, and two of them were chipped. That was the problem with fancy plates – they were far too delicate.

Frank arrived exactly when he said he would.

Mam was impressed and suggested that Dad had a lot to learn from this fine military example. She piled his plate high with boiled potatoes, cabbage and the most beautifully smelling steak in the world. Jack and Dad had hovered around the pan as Mam was frying it, breathing in the aroma and savouring every sniff.

"You not eating?" asked Frank, with a mouthful, noticing no one else had a plate.

Mam shook her head and told him that they'd already eaten.

"I'm full up," said Dad, and patted his belly with exaggerated slaps.

"Me too," smiled Jack. "I couldn't eat another cracker … er, I mean thing."

"Sorry," said Mam. "I hope that's not rude of us. So anyway, how's the steak?"

Dad leant in. "Aye, how is it? Is it as tender and tasty as it looks? Does it melt in your mouth?"

"Give the lad some space, man," said Mam, waving her hands, so Dad and Jack would back off. They were watching Frank's every mouthful.

"Aye," grinned Frank, putting on an accent, "it's … canny."

They all laughed.

"We'll make a Geordie of you yet," said Dad, before whispering, "but work on that accent! You do know we're not Welsh, don't you?"

The evening flew by. Everyone was under strict instructions to keep the mood light. Dad rolled out the jokes he kept for special occasions while Jack and Mam made an effort to laugh more than they would usually. Jack's tongue-twisters got them all in a muddle, especially Dad, who blamed his lack of teeth. It was Mam's clapping game that really confused them. No one managed to keep the correct pattern or rhythm. It was the most fun Jack had known since Gordon had left, but they couldn't put off the moment they were dreading.

Chapter 8
Saying goodbye

Lucy and the other barrage balloons were still swaying as they walked along the road, under the shadow of the battleship. Jack wore Frank's sailor's cap which proudly displayed the name HMS *Warspite*. Although it didn't quite fit, it wasn't far off. Jack wondered how long it would be before he could claim a similar cap of his own. It was a thought that would've usually excited him, but now he wasn't sure. Dad pointed out some of the parts of the ship he'd worked on, taking pride in what he, and so many others, had achieved in so little time. Even though no one was really listening, they all nodded politely.

The great Titan and the other cranes stood motionless, as if to attention, like a guard of honour ready to salute the old warship off on another adventure. It was eerily quiet. No hammering, riveting or welding. No clanking of armour panels or clattering of iron chains.

At the bottom of the bank, they saw Mr Osbourne, talking to a group of naval officers.

"That's the captain," Frank whispered, as he buttoned up his tunic and took back his cap. Jack noticed his dad straighten his back, while Mam pulled dangles of hair from her face.

"Ah, we thought you'd deserted, young man," said the captain, in a well-spoken voice.

Everyone's heart skipped a beat until the captain chuckled, and they realised he'd been joking. Frank stamped to attention and snapped a salute.

"These are the Colliers," said Mr Osbourne. "They've been looking after Frank here."

While the captain shook their hands, Mr Osbourne added, "Norman's one of the fellows who've restored your ship to full fighting glory. And Mary has a vital role at the armament factory up the road."

The captain was impressed. "On behalf of HMS *Warspite* and His Majesty's Forces, may I say how grateful we are for your skills and all you do for the war effort."

Mam brushed more hair from her face and made an awkward bowing motion. "Oh, my pleasure."

Dad shrugged. "No bother. It's what we do."

"The whole family is part of the war effort," continued Mr Osbourne. "Their son, Gordon, is in the infantry."

"I hope you're smarter than your brother, young man," said the captain, leaning towards Jack. "Maybe smart enough to join the navy, when the time comes?"

"Well, we'll see about that," said Mam, putting her arm around Jack.

"Right," snapped the captain. "Make your farewells brief. Lots to do."

While the captain and the other officers marched off, Mam, Dad, Jack and Frank made their way along the dock towards the gangplank that linked the ship to dry land.

Dad whispered to Mam with a smile, "Did you just curtsy to old Captain Barnacle there?"

"No, no, I didn't," said Mam, looking flustered. "And he's not 'old', I thought he looked very … dashing."

At the gangplank, Mam gave Frank a hug. "Right … well … this is it, then," she said, speaking over the low rumble of the battleship's engines. "It's been lovely having you to stay. We hope you'll – " Her hand covered her mouth as she fought back the tears.

Dad shook Frank's hand. "We hope you'll come back and visit us, when all this nonsense is over."

Frank nodded. "I'd like that. And I'm sorry about … all the fuss … I just – "

"No need to say sorry, pet," said Mam. "You're with friends here."

"Oh, I nearly forgot," said Frank, reaching

into his pocket and pulling out an envelope. "Would you post this for me, please?"

Dad took the letter from him, nodding. "And you're going to write lots more. So many your mam and dad will get sick of them."

Mam laughed. "They'll never get sick of them, never."

Jack had his farewell speech prepared. Ever since his brother had got on that train, he'd regretted not having the right words. So many times, he'd imagined that scene, and all the words he should have said. Tonight, Frank was going to get some of those words. But before Jack could speak, the sound of the air-raid siren screeched into life. Shouts from the ship called for Frank to get onboard.

"It'll be another false alarm," bellowed Dad, as Frank backed away up the gangplank as instructed. But this time, Jack wasn't so sure Dad was right. Further down the river towards the coast, the searchlights swept across the skies. Above the sound of the siren was something else. It was the purring of aircraft and the whistling of bombs falling from the sky.

"Action stations," shouted the captain, as he and the officers raced towards the warship. "Brace for impact!"

The dock was plunged into darkness as all the lights were turned off. Frank disappeared into the gloom towards his anti-aircraft gun. Sailors darted out from the darkness and headed for battle stations, which their training and experience had them well prepared for. Alarms, bells and whistles blared out from the ship. Murky smoke belched from ship's funnels, as the rumble of engines became more like thunder. Gusty winds from the river blew the blackened exhaust fumes along the dock, making the air dusty and fiery. Figures on the deck raced about, while orders and directions were shouted.

Jack's heart was thumping as they ran along the dock towards the nearest shelter. His mouth was dry, and his eyes were stinging from the vapours. Mam, Dad and Jack clung together, both in fear and to help each other along. Mr Osbourne was at the main gate frantically waving at them to hurry up.

They fell to the ground as intense explosions rocked the ship, pressing it hard against the dock walls. Metal and stone scraped together with an unnatural howl. The blast wave kicked up more dust and debris and hurled it at them. Jack wondered if the ship had been hit, but Dad sputtered, "That's the other side of the river."

Mam nodded. "The fuel depot."

Through the swirling smoke, the warship's silhouette was illuminated with a hauntingly flickering glow. The hum of aircraft became a roar, followed by a terrifying single-toned screech that went on and on, getting louder and louder, until ....

BOOM!

A moment of instant daylight blinded Jack. The fierce burst of sound shook his insides. Clumps of stone rained down, clattering onto the dock and clanging against the steel warship.

After a moment, Dad peered around. "Looks

like dry dock number two," he said in between gasps. "It's not being used. There shouldn't be anyone there."

It was less than 100 yards away. If the bomb had dropped just a moment later, things would've been very different. As they gathered themselves and prepared to run to the shelter, there was another noise to add to the chaos. The creaking, jarring sound of twisting and snapping metal came from above. There were no people at dry dock number two, but there was a crane. A crane that was now falling towards HMS *Warspite*.

Chapter 9
Mangled metal

Metal crashed into metal. A sharp, stinging blast of wind rammed into them, and they huddled together to shield themselves from any further impact. The intense crashing and creaking came to a drastic stop, and they slowly raised their heads. A fog of dust engulfed the battleship. Particles illuminated by the fire burning on the dry dock swirled around it like a swarm of angry fireflies. Mam, Dad and Jack checked each other over.

"Still in one piece!" Dad said. But that couldn't be said for something else.

One of the smaller cranes in the yard, Hector, was now lying crumpled and broken along the dry dock. Most of it had crashed onto unused parts of the dock, with some of it in the river. Unfortunately, the uppermost part, the jib, had smashed onto the front end of the ship and was rocking precariously on the mighty 15-inch gun turrets.

The gun placements, thought Jack. "What about Frank?" he shouted, pointing to the guns. "That's his post ... under the crane."

Without thinking, they bounded across the gangplank.

Some of the crew had gathered around the broken crane's jib and were trying to move it. It was still largely in one piece but too heavy to shift, and its mangled tip had smashed into a gun placement. A sailor clambered up to check and shouted, "Man down!"

Jack knew that wasn't good news.

"I can get the old Titan moving," shouted Mr Osbourne, in between gasps of dusty air. He was still on the dock, leaning against a barrier and clearly suffering, but still able to see what needed doing.

"Follow me," called Dad, as he raced back down the gangplank. Stopping at a brick storehouse, he rattled the door, but it was locked. He took one step back, then aimed a hefty kick, and the door broke open. By the time Jack, Mam and Mr Osbourne had joined him, Dad had dragged a selection of metal and leather straps out of the shed.

"I'll get the jib harnessed up," he said, "ready for the Boss to swing the Titan around and pick it off. And you both – " he turned to Jack and Mam, "need to get yourselves to the shelter."

Jack had no plans to leave. He looked up at the Titan's operator's cabin, which was high above their heads. Climbing up there would be tough.

"But," he said awkwardly, "how's Mr Osbourne going to get up there?"

Mr Osbourne grimaced as reality sunk in. It'd been many years since he'd been fit enough to make that climb. Mam pulled out a long strap and wrapped it around her shoulders while judging its strength and length.

"I'll get you up there, Mr Osbourne," she said, as she wrapped the strap around his waist. "I'll climb up the steps ahead of you. I'll take your weight and stop you from falling. It won't be pretty, or easy, but we'll get there."

Mr Osbourne gulped hard and nodded. There really was no other option.

"I'll help with harnessing the crane," said Jack, seeing the desperation on Dad's face.

Mam looked to the skies. The drone of aircraft had receded. "Maybe that's it for tonight?" she said to Dad. "Jack knows how to work a harness. He'll be a good help. But keep an eye on him."

Dad hesitated. He wanted to protect his family, but he also needed to finish this vital job.

Mr Osbourne put a hand on Dad's shoulder and said solemnly, "This ship must leave the yard, Norman. And it isn't just about deadlines; this ship is *needed* somewhere."

"For something big," said Jack, repeating both Frank and Gordon's words.

"All right, all right," snapped Dad. He gave Mam a hug and whispered in her ear, "Please be careful."

Mam gave Dad and Jack a quick kiss, and she yanked on the harness tied around Mr Osbourne's waist.

"Come on, then. I hope you haven't been cheating on your biscuits rations lately?"

Jack and Dad dragged the harnesses across the gangway while Mam and Mr Osbourne made their way to the first steps on the mighty Titan.

On the *Warspite*'s deck, Dad barked out instructions to the sailors clambering around the fallen crane. Jack was stunned how quickly they jumped into action, spreading out and untangling the harnesses. Although there were no yard lights due to the air raid, the decking was illuminated by the flickering glow of the burning fuel depot across the river and the flames from the base of the fallen crane.

Glancing across at the Titan, Jack could just see Mam's progress up the stairways and ladders and Mr Osbourne close behind her. He couldn't have been prouder of her. He felt the same about his dad as he watched him take charge of the situation. Even some of the more senior ranks had seen that Dad knew what he was doing and joined in without any questions. Jack showed some sailors how the straps should be wrapped around the crane and fitted together, just like his dad had showed him on previous visits to the yards. Once the harnesses seemed to be ready and in place, Dad tugged and checked every connection. *Everything is only as strong as its weakest part,* remembered Jack.

"Right," said Dad, turning his attention to the Titan. "Any sign of them?"

"They were just below the cabin a few minutes ago," Jack replied, but he couldn't see them anymore. Flickering light from the flames played tricks with his imagination. Shadows of the crane's steel girders quivered, giving the impression of movement. Each time Jack thought he could see them, his heart jumped, only to be frustrated.

Dad whispered, "Where are they?"

Jack's eyes drifted down the crane, fearing the worst. Squeezing his fists and hoping with all his might he wouldn't see Mam or Mr Osbourne any lower than he'd seen them last. Then a light blinked in the Titan's cabin. They'd made it!

Dad slapped a hand against his heart. "Your mam had me worried for a minute there."

Jack laughed with relief as the Titan groaned into life. Mr Osbourne wasn't wasting any time. Its enormous mechanical arm swept across the yard and came to a grinding halt over the *Warspite*. A giant hook at the end of the pulley swayed viciously about as it was lowered, and Dad shouted for everyone to clear the area. Anyone would be catapulted off the deck in an instant, if it hit them. In normal times, the movement of the Titan would've been graceful and controlled – but these weren't normal times. Climbing up onto the fallen crane, Dad was ready with a long, leather strap. He waited for the hook to swing as near as possible, then he hurled the strap towards it. On his first attempt, he caught the hook, like a cowboy lassoing a bad guy in a film Jack had seen at the cinema.

Once the harnesses were hooked up, everyone stepped well back. Dad stayed put. One of the sailors had lent him a torch, and he rapidly flashed it towards the Titan. More screeching and groaning came from the cables and straps as the monster crane took the strain. Hector seemed to call out in pain as its metallic bones bent under the tension. Everyone stepped even further back. Just when Jack thought it wasn't going to lift, there was a sudden judder, and the broken crane was released from the ship's deck. It clung for a second to the gun placement as if it didn't want to let go, before finally giving up its grip.

The loose crane lurched abruptly towards the ship's central tower, just a few feet from smashing into it. Dad yanked at a long, dangling strap, in an effort to control the jib's movement, but it was too much for him and he slid across the deck. Jack raced to help. He clung to his dad's waist, and they were dragged along like broken puppets, while some sailors jumped to grab the strap. More people holding on meant a collision with the crane and the ship was narrowly avoided, with only inches to spare. The Titan corrected its movement, and the remains of Hector were lifted safely away from the *Warspite* and back towards dry dock number two.

Dad patted the sailors on the back in gratitude but gave Jack a stern look. "You should've stayed back," he said, looking furious.

But Jack stood his ground. "I wasn't going to let you get hurt again."

The anger faded immediately, and Dad wrapped an arm around him.

"Frank!" Jack gasped, glancing to the gun placement and hoping his new friend was safe.

A figure silhouetted by the riverbank fire stood by the anti-aircraft gun and arched its back. It was Frank! He was helped down the stairway by fellow sailors, who had his arms draped over their shoulders.

"Glad to see you're still in one piece, bonny lad," said Dad, meeting him on deck.

"Just about," Frank said, with a pained smile. He pointed back towards his gun placement, "but I can't say the same about my post."

Jack noticed blood smeared across Frank's face.

"No sign of broken bones," said one of the sailors Frank was hanging on to, "but we'd better get you to the medical unit."

A senior officer ran past, stopping for a moment when he saw Dad and Jack.

"All civilians need to disembark," he shouted. "We're leaving the dock."

Horns and whistles blew, while the crew stomped about in their heavy boots. The roar of the engines grew louder, and more smoke spewed out from funnels. Jack was too worried about Frank to take much notice.

"But you're all right, aren't you?" Jack called out, as Frank was rushed away. The sailors disappeared into the ship before Frank had a chance to respond. Jack had been glad to see Frank emerge from under the wreckage of the crane, but shocked to see his bloodstained face. Frank was able to walk, with some help, and clearly able to talk. That must count for something … surely?

Dad had been looking at the gun station and was now coming back down the stairs. "We have to fix the armour plating," he panted, while his wide eyes darted about the dock. "I'll get the welding gear from the store."

"What?" replied Jack. "But the ship's leaving. We've got to go!"

Dad shook his head. "That's Frank's post. The crane knocked out the gun shield. I'm not letting him go back into action without that armour. And anyway, look … this ship isn't going anywhere just yet."

Jack's gaze followed where his dad was indicating and saw that there was yet another problem.

Not all of Hector had been removed by the Titan. Tangled girders from further down the jib had snapped off and twisted themselves onto the boundary fencing around the warship and the iron bollards of the dock. The wreckage had created a solid and unwanted anchoring link that even the mighty engines of the *Warspite* wouldn't be able to pull away from.

"The Titan?" asked Jack. "Can it lift that away as well?"

Dad shook his head. "It's too mangled. It'll pull a huge chunk off the ship. It's going to take cutting tools to break each girder." Dad wiped the sweat off his face. "Right. I'll tell you what we'll do. While I grab the welding gear, you get yourself as fast as you can to the shelter up the bank on Station Road near the Memorial Hall. There's a chance Sam or Kev are there. Or anyone from the yard. Tell them we need the cutting gear. Someone will know what to do."

Jack raced down the gangplank and along the dock, breathing in the thick exhaust gases mixed with fiery smoke from the explosions. His lungs burnt, his heart pounded and his legs ached, but he sprinted up the bank regardless. At the shelter, he burst in through the door, startling some children wrapped in blankets. He spluttered out what was happening and what was needed, not sure if he was making any sense.

A voice called out from the back as a few figures stood up. "Aye, lad, we can do that."

That was good enough for Jack. He'd done his part and now he had to head back to help Dad.

Dad was at the gun placement preparing the welding gear.

"Some of the blokes in the shelter are coming," Jack told him.

Dad nodded. "Good lad."

Jack had never been this close to a gun before. It was much bigger than he'd thought and must take a few people to operate. The scent of oil was lighter and sweeter than the usual heavy-duty aroma that wafted from the yard into his house. The gun itself had no obvious damage from the falling crane, but a portion of the thick shielding around it had been torn and bent so badly it was lying flat against the flooring.

"We'll need to pull this side of the armour plating up," explained Dad, "and then hold it in position while I weld it back in place."

"Get off my ship!" came a shout. It was the captain, climbing up the stairs towards them, and he was furious.

Chapter 10
Military offence

"We're fixing the gun shield," Dad shouted back at the captain. "It was damaged by the crane."

"I saw what happened from the Con," said the captain, pointing to the control tower. "I appreciate your efforts to clear the debris, but we're out of time for further repairs. You must disembark *right now*."

"But the armour around the gun placement … it won't be able to protect the lads," Dad told him.

"There are more important factors at work here," said the captain, failing to keep calm. He clearly wasn't used to being spoken back to. "That gun shield is not a part of operational necessity."

Jack couldn't believe it. This was where Frank, and his fellow sailors, were going to stand in times of danger. The ship was here to be repaired and that was what they were going to do. He fixed his gaze on the captain and shouted, "ALL parts matter!"

Dad nodded, but the captain couldn't contain his anger anymore. "This is MY ship, and you will leave *right this moment.*"

Dad pointed to the mangled crane holding the ship to the dock. "This ship is still anchored to our shipyard, and as long as that is the case, it's OUR ship."

The captain raised his hands in frustration. "I don't have time for this," he said, as he checked his watch. "You're all so hard-headed, you Geordies." He stepped back onto the stairs but turned to point at them and shouted through gritted teeth, "If you're still here when we depart, I'll throw you overboard myself." With that, he stormed off.

"We've got as long as it takes them to untangle the jib," said Dad, looking at the sailors pulling and kicking at the buckled metal strips.

They wouldn't be able to move much with just their hands, but Dad and Jack knew some cutting gear was on its way. Skilled workers with the right tools would have that removed in no time.

"We're not leaving until we've fixed this, right?" said Dad, and Jack nodded.

They both took hold of the armour plating that had partially snapped out of place and began to pull it up. It was still connected to the rest of the shield by a couple of inches of iron and it was heavier than Jack expected. He realised that the thick bulk of the plate was what made it good protection. Together, they slowly managed to bend it back, but it took a huge effort. Once it was where it needed to be, Jack braced himself to take the weight on his own, while Dad welded it. But as soon as Dad let go, it bent back too much. Jack became frustrated at not being strong enough to hold it on his own. Then suddenly, it stayed in place.

"I hope we're getting paid overtime for this!" said a voice in the darkness.

It was Mam! She had a hold of the plate, and

together they were able to keep it still while Dad ignited the welding tool. There'd not been time to grab any welding masks, so Dad squinted at the blinding light, while Jack and Mam squeezed their eyes shut and turned away. Jack could still see the brightness through his eyelids and feel the specks of molten metal splatter against his face.

There was an instant stench of red-hot iron. After a minute or so, Dad told them they could release their grip. The heavy plate, which

had taken so much effort to hold, was now firmly fixed into position. The next time Jack watched the welding activities of the yard from the safety of his bedroom window, he'd be more impressed.

Dad made some further adjustments by striking the armour with a huge hammer, making it bong like Big Ben on New Year's Eve. While he finished off the welding, and then filed some edges down, Jack saw that the cutting team had started dismantling the remaining parts of the crane. Then he noticed that it wasn't just a few of the men he'd seen getting ready in the shelter, or the sailors desperate to release their ship from its unwanted tether. The dock was filling up with people of all shapes and sizes, and of all ages and abilities. There were some even wearing pyjamas and slippers. It was a well-known

fact around the town that the *Warspite* had an important deadline. News must have quickly spread around the shelters, and even though the "all clear" hadn't sounded, everyone wanted to help.

Jack was amazed at how quickly they organised themselves into a long line. Once the cutting team had sliced off parts of the crane, the smaller sections were passed down the line, while the bulkier items were dragged out of the way by smaller groups. In no time at all, there was a cheer from the crowd around the crane. *That could only mean one thing,* thought Jack. The battleship was free … and it was about to set sail.

Chapter 11
Into the darkness

Jack pulled at Dad's jacket. "We need to go!"

"Just a bit more work on these rough edges," said Dad, running his hand over the panel.

Mam grabbed the welding gear in one hand and Dad with the other. "Those edges will have to stay rough," she said, pulling him down the stairs as the ship's horn let out an ear-piercing blare. The ship rocked as the remaining ropes and chains holding it to the dock were removed, and they were forced to stagger about as they ran across the deck. Sailors at the gangway began winding it in.

"Wait!" shouted Jack, who was in no mood to be thrown into the Tyne by the ship's captain. Luckily, the sailors saw them, but furiously waved their arms to make them speed up. They held the gangway in place for just a few seconds more. Jack, Mam and Dad raced across the clattering walkway which was unsecured and far wobblier than before. Jack caught a glimpse of the sparkling river below and wished he'd not looked down. Once on the dock, the three of them fell into the arms of those that'd come to help.

A cheer rang out from the crowd, and Mr Osbourne laughed, "I didn't think you were going to make it."

Jack had thought the same. He was relieved to be on solid ground, as the gap between the dock and the warship suddenly became huge. Engines roared, smoke belched from the funnels, and horns blasted their farewell. One more thought sprang to Jack's mind … Frank. He'd not said goodbye to Frank.

Jack pushed his way through the crowd on the dock and followed the ship. He kept his eyes on the *Warspite* drifting into the river as he ran. He tried to see faces in the figures on the ship, hoping to see Frank but knowing it was useless as he'd still be in the medical unit. He raced along the dock like he'd raced along the platform after Gordon's train. Feeling the same heartache, the same hopelessness.

Fallen remains of the bombed crane brought an end to Jack's running. This was as far as he could go. Straining his eyes to see through the smoke and darkness, he could just make out some sailors standing at the rear of the ship. Maybe they were taking one last look at their home country before going to who-knows-where? One of the figures moved their arms in an unusual manner. Jack's heart nearly burst. Their arms arched up and down at their sides. It was too far to see a face, but the arms kept repeating that motion. It was Frank. It must be! Jack copied the motion and jumped up as high as he could in the hope he might be seen too. The outline of the figure quickly faded as it was swallowed up by the distance and the smoke.

Footsteps behind made Jack turn. It was Mam and Dad.

"I saw Frank," gasped Jack, breathless and exhausted. "He's all right." But then the thought of what was waiting for Frank out there hit him hard, and he added in a whisper, "For now."

Mam put her arm around him. "I suppose that's all we can hope for any of us," she said, "to be all right ... for now."

"Do you think we did the right thing?" asked Dad. "He could've been safe in the countryside now, instead of – "

"We did all we could," replied Mam. "It's up to them now."

"Come on then, lad," said Dad to Jack. "It's past all our bedtimes."

Jack told them he'd be a minute and let them head back. He wanted to take in every last moment of watching the Grand Old Lady, HMS *Warspite*, sail out of the Tyne and into the war.

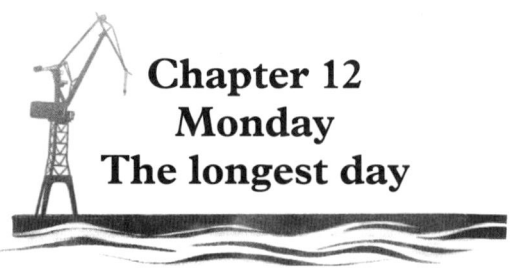

Chapter 12
Monday
The longest day

Mondays were always long and horrible, but this was a particularly gruelling one for everyone along the river. In the aftermath of the air raid, news and rumours slowly spread around town. Thankfully, for now, there were no reports of deaths or serious injuries, but the shock would linger for a long time. There was a fear that air raids would become a regular event again, just as they had been a few years ago.

The armament factories had been spared any bombing, which was a huge relief to all. A direct hit would have been disastrous, not just to the factory, but to the whole surrounding area. The families living in the nearby houses would be having sleepless nights for the foreseeable future.

Mam and her fellow workers completed their usual Monday shift but used their breaks and sometime afterwards to visit nearby air-raid shelters. They made sure they were clean and tidy, and repaired minor breakages. Chairs and blankets had been donated by many, no doubt as the result of those who spent an uncomfortable, chilly night sitting on concrete floors. There were constant offers of cups of tea from grateful older folks watching from their front doorsteps. Mam politely refused most offers, but made sure she didn't refuse any biscuits, which she stuffed into her overall pockets for later.

Once a ship had left the yards, there was always a huge clear-up operation, but a bomb landing in dry dock number two and demolishing a crane, was a whole new level of clear up. Dad and a full shift of yard workers removed as much debris from the fallen crane as they could, to make the main dock ready and safe for another visitor. The dry dock had been closed off, leaving the crumpled remains of the crane a sombre sight – a reminder to everyone of that night.

Due to the air raid running past 11 o'clock

in the evening, Jack and all the children in the area had gone to school at the later time of half past ten that morning. Jack had posted Frank's letter; he'd dropped it into a post box with a mixture of sorrow and hope.

During the air raid, an incendiary bomb had landed on the school's football field and set fire to the wooden changing block. *Typical*, Jack thought. That was the one part of school he enjoyed. Jack spent most of the day helping to sort out burnt and damaged bits of wood from the wood that might be used again for something else. Anything that could be salvaged was considered a small victory. He was glad to not be doing lessons and the dreaded equations, but it was seriously hard work, and his hands quickly became battered and bruised. The school day flew by, and afterwards he met up with a few friends to talk about the events of the night before. They all told of the bangs and crashes they'd heard from inside their shelters and how excitingly scary it had all been. Then Jack described his night to a wide-eyed and open-mouthed audience. No one could compete with that.

On the way home, Jack met Mam on their street. He felt the breeze from the river again, now that there was no ship present. Instead of smelling refreshing, the breeze had a tang of diesel and oil. Smoke drifted up from the fuel depot on the other bank. The barrage balloons were still gently bobbing about and ready for another possible air raid. As they reached the house, a wave of exhaustion swept over them both. Jack's legs felt like lead, and his back felt as broken as poor old Hector.

Then they noticed the shattered windows to many of the houses nearest the yards, clearly a result of the blast the night before. Luckily, all their own windows were still intact, but their neighbours hadn't been so fortunate. Some of the clearing up had already been done, and many windows had been boarded using floorboards and anything else to hand. Mr and Mrs Lachut were sweeping up broken glass, so Mam went to help. Their front window had only been cracked by the bomb blast but had finally shattered after Mr Lachut had slammed the front door shut.

"I don't know why he has to bang the door so hard," Mrs Lachut chuckled, while Mr Lachut shrugged sheepishly.

"Get yourselves inside," said Mam, seeing that they were struggling. "We'll sort this out for you."

The couple objected, but no one argued with Mam for too long without losing. As she picked up the larger shards of glass, Mam cut herself. She watched as the red blood mingled with the dirt and grime on her fingers.

"Hey!" came a shout from behind them. "Have you been breaking windows with that football again, young lady?"

It was Dad. He looked like he'd spent the day down a mine; the only clean part of him was the single tooth they could see as he smiled. Seeing the blood on Mam's finger, he untucked a flap of his shirt and tore off a strip, then gently bandaged up her injury. They cleared up the glass and fixed some cardboard from a box of condensed milk over the window frame. It would be enough to stop the breeze for the moment, until it got properly repaired another day. They stuck their heads into the Lachut's front room, just to make sure they'd settled, but saw Mrs Lachut crying in her armchair; Mr Lachut had dropped the kettle in the kitchen and had made everything wet. The events of the night before had clearly shaken them badly.

Mam and Dad took charge. They made cups of tea and something for the Lachuts to eat, while Jack got to tell his story again. Not wanting to leave the elderly couple in an anxious state, they stayed to chat, while sharing some dusty biscuits from Mam's pockets.

It was as they were chatting that Dad noticed a magazine on a small table next to Mrs Lachut's chair. He gestured with his head to point it out to Mam and Jack, and whispered, "The curious case of the mysterious steak has been solved."

When they saw it, they smiled – it was a torn copy of *Knitting for Victory*.

When they finally got back home, Mam and Dad slumped together into the big chair after Jack made them a cup of tea. In the short time it took to make, he returned to find them both holding hands, soundly snoring. The framed picture of  Gordon was cradled in Mam's lap. Jack perched himself on the arm of the chair to snuggle in, too. *They might as well get some sleep while they can,* Jack thought. *Who knows what will happen to them tonight? Who knows what's going to happen to Frank and Gordon?* Sliding his hand in between theirs, so that the dirt, bruises, cuts and scrapes all blended together, it was impossible to tell whose fingers were whose.

Chapter 13
Tuesday 6th June 1944
Something big

The next morning, news slowly trickled in of a huge military operation in France. In the early hours, Operation Neptune had been activated and the largest seaborne invasion in history had begun.

HMS *Warspite* was the first battleship in action.

Its duty was to provide bombardment cover for Allied soldiers landing in Normandy as they stormed the beaches to battle the might of the German army. During those crucial first few hours, it was attacked by enemy aircraft. Onboard, anti-aircraft guns responded to the assault. One recently welded gun shield was hit by enemy fire but protected the sailors behind it. This enabled the heroic operators to turn and face their enemy, and they managed to target and strike the aircraft, so it couldn't damage its intended objective: the 15-inch guns.

It was these 15-inch guns that pounded the enemy on land and protected the Allied forces on the beach. One shell fired from the *Warspite* hit an enemy machine gun emplacement just as the 3rd Infantry Division were advancing towards it, completing their desperately dangerous campaign across the beach. The destruction of that machine gun

post no doubt saved the lives of all members of that division, including a scared but determined young private named Gordon Collier.

This day became known as D-Day. It was the start of the end of the Second World War. The brave military personnel are rightly remembered for their actions that day, and on the many days that followed. But it is sometimes forgotten that many, many other people played their part too, and *every part matters*.

Book talk questions

How did you feel at the end of the book?

What do you think the town's contributions to the war effort show about ordinary people during wartime?

How does Jack's perspective on the war evolve throughout the story?

Which character did you identify most with?

What do you think is the most important message for readers to take away from Jack's experience?